TICK TOCK AND TREACHERY

COZY MYSTERY TAILS OF ALASKA, BOOK 6

PATTI BENNING

SUMMER PRESCOTT BOOKS PUBLISHING

Copyright 2019 Summer Prescott Books

All Rights Reserved. No part of this publication nor any of the information herein may be quoted from, nor reproduced, in any form, including but not limited to: printing, scanning, photocopying, or any other printed, digital, or audio formats, without prior express written consent of the copyright holder.

**This book is a work of fiction. Any similarities to persons, living or dead, places of business, or situations past or present, is completely unintentional.

1

Angie Seaver walked into her parents' room carrying two cups of tea. She sat them both down on her mother's vanity before turning to see the older woman standing over her bed, her hands on her hips as she looked at the pile of clothes sitting next to her suitcase.

"Need some help?" she asked.

"I always over pack. Your father asked me to get everything in one suitcase this time. I'm not sure how I'll manage."

"Well, you're going to be gone for five nights, right?"

"Right. Five nights. We're coming back on the evening of the sixth day."

"So just count out five pairs of everything, throw in an extra pair in case something gets dirty, and call it good."

"You make it sound easy, but what if we go out to eat somewhere nice? I should bring a dress. Or if the weather takes a turn for the worse, I'll wish I had some of my warmer sweaters."

"You'll be fine," Angie said. "You'll be in the city, and you probably won't be spending much time outside anyway. Plus, we may live in Alaska, but you're not going to need a parka in the middle of summer. Just bring a jacket. Is everything else okay? You seem nervous."

"I just hope everything goes well. Your father has his hopes up so high about this new treatment, and I know we're both going to be crushed if I'm not eligible for it."

"I'm sure everything will work out as it's meant to," she replied. She stepped closer and gave her mother a hug. "Now, let's get you packed up and ready to go."

They spent a few minutes digging through her mother's clothes. Angie folded the pants and shirts as they were handed to her and put them in the suitcase, then, before she forgot, she went around to the nightstand to unplug her mother's phone charger and tucked it into one of the bag's pockets as well.

"Are you bringing your laptop?"

"No, I don't really see a reason to. I'll leave it here."

"All right. What's next? Makeup? Toiletries?"

"All of that. That reminds me, I do want to bring my hairdryer. I'll get started packing all of that up. Can you run out to the living room and grab my purse? I want to switch it out with a bigger one."

She did as she was asked, and helped her mother pack up the last few items. Somehow, they managed to fill both the large suitcase and her mother's oversized purse. Angie eyed the smaller carry-on sized suitcase her father had packed that morning, which was sitting by the bedroom door, and smiled. It was a reminder of the fact that in some ways her parents were very different people, but somehow they had managed to make it work for decades.

"I'm going to miss you guys," she said, sitting down to drink her now cold tea. "You'll call me when you get there, won't you?"

"Of course," her mother said. "And we'll miss you too, Angie. You sure you'll be all right taking care of everything here?"

"I'll be fine. Dad already left me a list about everything I have to do for the dogs, and I know where the cat food is for Chess and Checkers. Everything will be great here."

"And you're sure you're okay working an extra shift at the diner this weekend?"

"I'm sure, Mom," Angie said. "I don't mind the extra work, and I wouldn't want to ask Betty to work two extra shifts. She's already covering for Dad on Sunday."

"I just feel so bad about leaving you in charge of all of this while we go out of town," the older woman said with a sigh.

"I moved out here to help you and Dad," Angie pointed out. "This is what I'm doing. Don't feel bad about it. I missed out on a lot of chances to help you guys, and I want to make up for it. Don't worry about anything. Just enjoy your trip with Dad, relax while you're at the medical center, and come home feeling better."

She heard dogs barking outside, and gave her mother one final smile before draining the last of the tea from her cup and heading for the door, calling back to tell her mother that she was going to go see if her father needed any help putting the dogs away.

Petunia, their elderly red and white husky who had retired from a life as a sled dog and was living out her retirement years indoors, was already waiting by the front door, dancing around with excitement at the sound of the sled dog team returning. Angie bent down to pet her.

"Do you want to go out and say hi to everyone?" she asked. She got a sharp bark in response, and chuckled as she slid her feet into the mud boots that were waiting by the door.

She opened the front door to let the dog run out ahead of her. Her father was just pulling into the yard in his old pickup truck. He was towing an ATV, and in the bed of the truck was a dog box, with eight compartments for the dogs to ride comfortably in. He pulled to a stop between the house and the barn and shut the engine off, getting out of the driver's side door and waving at Angie before bending down to greet the overly enthusiastic Petunia.

"This is nice, two of my favorite girls coming out to say hi to me."

"Your other favorite girl is inside finishing up her packing," Angie said. "Mom's just about ready to go. Do you need help with any of this?" She waved her hand, encompassing the dogs and ATV all at once.

"If you want to get the dogs put away, I will put the four-wheeler and trailer back in the barn," he said. "Take Oracle to the dog yard on the leash. Last time I had him out off leash, he took off like an arrow, and I don't want to spend an hour tracking him down before we go. The others should just run up to the gate."

She followed his instructions, grabbing Oracle's leash from the cab and opening the door to his box. She clipped the leash on him then let him jump down. She opened the other doors afterward and the rest of the team leapt out, taking a moment to mob Petunia in greeting before Angie gave a sharp whistle and started toward the dog yard.

They raced ahead of her, piling up at the gate and getting in her way as she pulled it open. It took her a few minutes to sort them all out and hook them up in the right spots. When she was done, she double checked that everyone had fresh water, then called to Petunia and left the dog yard, latching the gate securely behind her. While she had told her mother that she wasn't worried about taking care of all the dogs while they were gone, it was only partially true. With nearly twenty dogs on their property, it was going to be a lot of work to get done early in the mornings before she went into the diner, and a lot of work at night too. She hadn't raced a team of sled dogs in years, and wasn't confident enough to take them out on her own, so their exercise would be limited to a few runs in the big fenced in yard that they had for that purpose.

Maybe Malcolm can come over and run a few of them with his team, she thought as she walked back toward her father's truck. He was just finishing up putting the ATV and the trailer he had away in the barn. The barn was filled with all of the gear he needed for his hobby of mushing. There were various sleds, dry land carts, and of course the four wheeler, along with rows of harnesses and gang lines hanging from the walls. He had amassed all of this gear over his entire life, and she knew that there was tens of thousands of dollars worth of equipment, not even counting the large freezers where he stored the dogs' food.

"There we go," he said, patting the four wheeler fondly before stepping out of the barn and shutting the big front doors. He seemed happy, which told Angie that it had been a good run. She knew that he would miss the dogs over the coming days. Other than her mother and the diner, the dogs had been the main focus of his life for the past decade. She knew he loved them, probably almost as much as he loved his own children.

"How did it go this morning?" she asked as the two of them walked toward the house.

"It went pretty well. I met up with a couple of the guys and we practiced passing head on. The team this year is mostly young dogs, so it's good for them to get used to it. They did well. Oracle is shaping up to be a great leader."

"That's wonderful news," she said.

"I found something neat while we were stopped for a break," he said, pausing to dig through his pocket. He took out what looked like an old, dirty wristwatch and handed it over to her. Angie looked over it in puzzlement.

"That's pretty cool," she said at last, wiping some of the dirt off of the face with her thumb. The watch was gold, as was the wristband, though it was caked with dirt.

He chuckled. "I think it's real gold. It looks pretty old, it's probably been out there for a few years at least. Look at the back, it looks like there's something inscribed there."

She flipped it over. Sure enough, there was something scratched into the metal on the back, but it was impossible to read. "It's an interesting mystery," she said.

"Would you mind seeing if you could get it cleaned up for me while we're gone? I think the jeweler would be able to do it." He shook his head. "I can't believe that man is still working. He was old when I bought your mother's engagement ring from him all those years ago. He must be close to a hundred now."

"I can take it over to him after work tomorrow," she said, opening the front door and stepping inside. "I'll let you know how it turns out."

"Thanks, Ange," he said. "I better get cleaned up and ready to go. Your mother and I have a long few days ahead of us."

2

After her parents left, Angie spent another hour getting ready for her date that evening. She and Malcolm Miles had been seeing each other pretty much since she moved back to town. He was a newcomer to town himself, and lived only about a mile down the road from her parents' house.

She had actually met him through her parents. He and her father had befriended each other before she moved back home, and her father was teaching him the ropes of owning and caring for sled dogs. Malcolm had his own small team of dogs, mostly inherited from other mushers in the area, and was quickly sinking deep into the hobby.

Sometimes the fact that he had known her parents longer than she had known him struck her as a little bit odd. It was a strange sort of normal to come home and find her boyfriend working with her dad on a project in the yard, or find out that he had been invited over for dinner and no one had thought to tell her. Still, somehow, it worked. He was a family friend, she supposed that she was lucky that everyone liked him, since he was over there quite a bit.

Thursday night was their date night, since Friday nights he drove down to Anchorage to pick up his two daughters. He had them almost every weekend, and spent his Saturdays and Sundays showing them around town and giving them the time of their lives. So far Angie hadn't met them in an official capacity, though she did see them once or twice a month when she worked a Saturday morning shift at the diner, and served them her famous smiley face pancakes.

They were going out to a local steakhouse tonight, a

place that had been the location of the majority of their dates. Restaurants were few and far between in Lost Bay, Alaska, and Angie knew that any date that she had at the diner would only serve as fodder for gossip amongst all the other employees. Besides, it felt weird to be served food at a place where she spent most of her time working.

Malcolm was early that evening, which didn't surprise her. Her hair was only half done when she opened the front door for him, letting him inside. He greeted Petunia, who was falling over herself in excitement to see him. Dogs seemed to love him from the get-go, which she supposed was good, given his choice in hobbies. Some people just seemed to have a natural gift with animals. She was good with them, but she just didn't have the magic touch that Malcolm and her father did.

"Hey," he said with a grin as he straightened up, brushing some stray dog fur from his pants. It was a losing battle, since Petunia was still sitting pressed against his leg.

"Hey," she replied, leaning in to share a quick kiss with him. She felt a tingle of electricity at the simple touch, and suddenly realized just how much she was looking forward to their date. "A pettier woman might be jealous that the dog is the one who got the more exuberant greeting."

"She practically threw herself into my arms," he said. "I'm not about to deny this pretty girl a good petting when she's so excited to see me." He reached down to stroke Petunia's ears. Angie laughed.

"I guess that's a good point. Plus, I get steak for dinner. She doesn't." She paused, considering. Petunia actually probably *would* get steak for dinner, since Angie would likely bring home leftovers. "Anyway, I've got to go finish getting ready. Make yourself at home like usual. I'll be ready to go in about ten minutes."

She left Malcolm in the living room, knowing that he was nearly as familiar with the house as she was, and quickly finished her hair and makeup. Her stomach was growling, and she could hardly wait to get to the restaurant. She was already thinking about what appetizer she wanted to get.

When she walked back into the living room, she found Malcolm petting one of the cats, while trying to keep Petunia back with the other hand. He was laughing, and she felt her heart flutter at the sight. Something about having him there was just so… right. They didn't have an epic romance like she read about in books and had seen in movies, filled with drama and sweeping declarations of passion. Instead, it was like they just fit. Like they were two puzzle pieces that fit together so well, it was almost like they had always been in each other's lives.

"I'm all set," she said softly, interrupting the scene in front of her. He turned around to look at her, and his face lit up.

Rising from the couch, he walked toward her and

they headed for the front door together. She paused at the closet to grab her favorite pair of flats.

"What's this?" he asked.

She looked up and saw him eying the old watch her father had found, which was still lying on the end table near the door where she had left it when she came in.

"It's something my dad found while he was out running the dogs today," she told him, hopping on one foot while she slipped her shoe on. "You can look at it, if you want. He asked me to get it cleaned for him while he and my mom are gone. I thought I'd run it in to the jeweler after work tomorrow."

He picked it up, turning the watch over in his hands and squinting at the back of it. "I know someone who loves restoring old pieces like this. I could take it to him, if you'd like. I think the jeweler in town just sends things away for serious restoration. It would be neat if we could figure out who it belongs to and then return it to them. It looks expensive."

She shrugged, picking up her purse. "Go ahead. I trust your judgment when it comes to people. As long as he'll get it back to us in the next couple of days, that would be fine."

He slipped the watch into his pocket. "I'll bring it to him tomorrow. This is a neat find. Your dad got lucky."

They walked out the front door together. Angie paused to lock it behind them, then followed Malcolm to his car. "I hope your guy can get the inscription cleaned up. That's really the part I'm most interested in. I've never really been a watch person myself, and I've got no clue about the value of it. I bet there's a bunch of old stuff out there, though. This town was booming during the gold rush."

"We should head out with a metal detector sometime. Maybe I can take my girls out treasure hunting sometime this summer." He started the car and began driving down the long driveway. "Actually, that might be a fun thing for all of us to do together. If you'd like to join us."

It took Angie a moment to fully realize what he had said. "Wait, all of us? You want me to meet them?"

"Well, you've already technically met them. But I'd like to introduce you to them as my... lady friend. That might need some work, actually. We can discuss what we want to tell them about us. We don't have to do it yet, if you don't want to or if you feel like you're not ready."

"Malcolm, are you kidding? I'd love to formally be introduced to your kids as someone other than the person who makes them smiley face pancakes. Are *you* sure you're ready? It's going to be a big step."

"I've been thinking about it for a while," he said, keeping his eyes on the road as they drove toward town. "We've been seeing each other for a few months. Our relationship seems solid, at least to me. I can't see either of us ending things soon. If I'm wrong, please let me know."

"I feel the same as you about everything you just said."

His shoulders seemed to relax a bit. "Good. You're a big part of my life, and so are my kids. I don't like having to keep two major areas of my life completely separate. I think they should get to know you, and you them. I mean, they're going to love you. You're amazing. And I might be biased, but they're pretty amazing too."

Angie chuckled. "Hey, didn't I just tell you that I trust your judgment about people? I'm sure I'm going to adore your kids."

Malcolm looked over at her, giving her a quick smile. "This is going to be great. It's definitely time. How would you feel about spending some time with us next weekend? I'd do it this weekend, but I do want to talk to their mother first — we try to keep each other in the loop, and I think taking a big step like this and bringing someone else into the girls' lives is something I should tell her about first. I wanted to talk to you before I bring it up with her, though."

"I understand. That will give me more time to prepare, anyway." She wasn't sure exactly how she was going to prepare, but she definitely didn't want to do something so important without having a game plan. What if she messed up? What if she made his kids hate her? She had never dated someone with children before, and was in completely uncharted waters with this. "You'll see me at the diner Saturday, though. I'm taking my dad's shift this weekend."

He chuckled. "The girls will be glad. Your pancakes are the best."

3

The problem with Thursdays being date nights was that Angie had to wake up early the next morning. Getting home at midnight, only to wake up at five the next morning was not her idea of a good time. She groaned, hitting the alarm's off button with more force than was necessary, and then turned her head to look at Petunia, who was laying stretched out beside her.

"I know, it's a bit earlier than usual, but I've got to take care of all the other dogs and feed the cats. You can keep sleeping if you want."

The dog closed her eyes as if in response to her

words, and Angie chuckled. She threw the blanket off and forced herself to her feet, promising herself that she would go to bed early that night. It would be strange, being here without her parents for so long, but it would be a bit like a mini-vacation. She loved her parents, but it was always nice to get some alone time when she lived with other people.

She turned on the coffee maker — something her father usually did; she had gotten used to having piping hot coffee waiting for her in the mornings — and stumbled outside to take care of the dogs while it gurgled away. Thankfully, her father had pre-portioned the food, so it was just a matter of filling the dishes, dragging the cart outside, passing out the bowls, then repeating the process after cleaning and refilling the water dishes. Cleaning the yard would have to wait until that afternoon; there was no way she was going to get that done before work.

Going through her morning routine felt strangely lonely without her parents there. She was thankful that she had Petunia to keep her company, and Chess and Checkers, who usually spent their mornings napping on her parents' bed, wound around her ankles as she did her hair. She realized that this was going to be a strange few days for the animals too. Usually, her mother was home most of the day and her father was in and out as he cared for the dogs. Spending the day alone while she was at the diner wasn't going to be very fun for them.

"I'm sorry, guys," she said as she slipped her purse's strap over her shoulder and cracked the front door open. "I'll be back in a few hours, I promise. Be good while I'm gone."

With that, she left, locking the door behind her and getting into the old vehicle that her father had given her for the duration of her stay. It started with a comfortingly familiar rumble, and then she was off.

The diner was the same as ever. She loved the early mornings, even if she didn't like waking up for them. There was something comforting and peaceful about the opening routine. She had gotten in the habit of skipping breakfast at home in order to make herself something at the diner, and usually had enough time to get everything ready for the day and finish her meal before anyone else got there.

Theo was working with her that morning, and got there just a couple of minutes before they opened. He covered up a yawn as he reached for the coffee pot, and she laughed.

"My father keeps asking all of us non-morning people to take the opening shift. We should stage a revolt."

"He'd probably just schedule us to open even earlier out of revenge. He's mentioned trying to catch the 5 AM crowd before."

Angie shuddered. "I might actually revolt if he decided to start opening the diner two hours earlier.

I'd have to wake up a little after three. Anything before five in the morning is the middle of the night as far as I'm concerned..."

They unlocked the front doors together, and moments later had their first customer; a regular who was there at seven-thirty sharp almost every morning. Angie returned to the kitchen to get him his coffee without being asked; she had been there long enough to know that his order never changed.

The morning passed quickly, the morning rush of harried nine to five workers fading into the more relaxed brunch crowd around ten. Angie and Theo managed to keep up with the demand, just barely. It was a relief when Betty got there at eleven. Betty had been working at the diner pretty much as long as there had been a diner, and Angie was convinced that she knew the place even better than her father did.

"Whew, busy morning?" the older woman asked as

she walked into the kitchen. Angie was making an omelet at the stove, and didn't dare take her eyes off of the eggs as she replied.

"You know how there's usually a lull around ten? That didn't happen today. Poor Theo's been running back and forth non-stop pretty much since we opened. I haven't had a chance to take a break either. All the orders are starting to sound the same to me."

Betty chuckled. Out of the corner of her eye, Angie could see her pulling on her apron. She folded the omelet in half and slipped it onto a plate, then finally put the spatula down and groaned. The older woman walked over to her and made a shooing motion.

"You go take that plate out to the customer and tell poor Theo to go take his break. Once he's done, it's your turn. You look dead on your feet, and food always tastes better when it's made by someone chipper."

"I'm not sure that's true," Angie said, but she grabbed the plate and headed toward the door, nonetheless. It was almost impossible to argue with Betty when she decided to take control of things.

A short break was all that she needed to get back in the swing of things. With Betty there, she was able to alternate between working in the kitchen and waiting tables, which took some of the pressure off of Theo as well.

By the time the lunch rush ended, all of the burgers and sandwiches were starting to look pretty darn good to Angie. Being on her feet and working around food all day made her hungry by the time the afternoon hit, even if she had eaten a good breakfast. After saying goodbye to Theo, whose shift was over, she told Betty she was going to take a few minutes to herself and fired up the grill for a burger of her own.

A few minutes later, she was seated at the counter by the register out front with a steaming burger and fries sitting in front of her.

She bit into the burger, which had sautéed mushrooms and onions, melted Swiss cheese, and just a hint of honey mustard sauce on it, and closed her eyes in bliss.

"Have you heard from your parents yet?" Betty asked, sliding into the seat next to her with a bowl of broccoli cheddar soup and some fries. There was an elderly man on her other side, who gave her a friendly nod — Betty knew just about everyone in town — and a family of three a few seats down from Angie. Their young son was tugging on his mother's arm and pointing at Angie's plate, ignoring his own chicken nuggets. The man sitting on the other side of her looked to be much older than his wife, enough so that Angie would have wondered at their relationship if he hadn't leaned over to kiss her on the cheek as she watched. He then turned to an elderly woman on his other side and said something to her that made her smile. His mother? Angie wondered. She recognized her as a regular, but didn't know her name.

"Angie?"

She jolted, realizing that Betty had asked her a question. She dabbed at her lips with a napkin before she spoke. "They called me when they got in late last night. They said they'd call again today or tomorrow to let me know how things are going."

"I'm glad they're doing this. I hope the doctors can help your mother. She's such a kind woman. Life has really thrown her some curveballs."

That's one way of putting it, Angie thought. Her mother's youngest daughter had passed away before she reached twenty years of age, and less than a decade later, she had been diagnosed with Parkinson's disease, which had developed aggressively. It wasn't fair, but Angie had come to terms with that long ago. Very little in life was. People could only do the best they could with what they were given, and Angie thought her mother was doing a wonderful job with her lot in life.

"I don't think I ever really realized it before, but she and my dad are both pretty happy people, despite everything they've been through. I really admire them for it."

Betty nodded. "You've got a good family. I know you know that, but not everyone's so lucky." She looked sad for a moment, then perked up. "How's your father doing with being away from the diner all this time? It's strange not seeing him here. He usually works himself to the bone."

"I think the break will be good for him," Angie said. "It's not quite a vacation, but it's the closest thing to one they've had for a long time. He was in a pretty good mood when he left, though that could have just been because of the watch."

"The watch?"

"He found an old gold wristwatch at the park on his last run with the dogs. Malcolm is taking it to get cleaned. There was something inscribed on the back, but it was too worn and dirty for any of us to make out. My dad loves old things like that, I think he probably thought it was good luck or something."

The man on the other side of Betty got up, placing a few crumpled bills on the counter next to his plate and nodding to them. "Have a nice day, Mr. Lowery," Betty said, giving him a cheerful smile as she slipped into her waitress voice. The man grunted a reply and was out the door before she even reached for the bills.

"That was odd," Angie muttered, watching as Betty counted the money then folded the bills in half and tucked them under her plate to be put in the register when she was done with her meal.

"Oh, Mr. Lowery has always been a bit odd. He lost his wife, you know, a good twenty years ago. He hasn't been the same since."

Angie nodded and turned back to her burger, almost jumping out of her seat when she saw that the child from further down the counter had somehow managed to sneak up on her and was now sitting right next to her, his chubby hand reaching for her plate to snatch away a couple of fries. She tried to cover her gasp up by coughing into her elbow. The young mother hurried over, apologizing.

"He's at the stage where he's just curious about everything," she explained as she tugged the boy away. "If I take my eyes off him for even one second…"

"It's fine," Angie laughed, waving it off. "I'm not usually so jumpy. And if he wants more fries, I can run back and grab some. We offer bottomless fries for all meals."

"Thanks, but we're trying to get Mikey to eat his nuggets. A growing boy needs more than just potatoes."

Angie turned back to her burger and her conversation with Betty. After the interruption, the topic changed to their plans for the upcoming week, and Angie found herself once again looking forward to all the alone time she was going to get while her parents were out of town.

4

One of the many things that Angie appreciated about her job was the fact that she was almost always off by three in the afternoon on the days that she worked. Sometimes she would stop in town and get coffee with her friend, Maggie, other times she would go shopping or take a walk in one of the parks. That afternoon, she just went home. With all of the dogs to take care of, she had a lot to do. Her father usually spent his mornings with them, so they were probably wondering where everyone had gone and why they had been left alone for so long. They would be bored, and she wanted to take them out to the bigger yard where they could run free and play together.

It took her until five to finish taking care of the dogs, which included refilling all of the small kiddie pools in the big yard for them to splash around in and tossing a ball for everyone until her arm felt like it was about to fall off. She fed them just before she went in. It was a little bit early for their evening meal, but as far as the dogs were concerned, it couldn't happen soon enough.

She retreated indoors with Petunia, heading to the kitchen where the older dogs' kibble was kept and giving her a scoop in the food bowl. She was interrupted by a meowing and straightened up to see both cats standing in the kitchen doorway, watching her expectantly.

"Don't worry, I didn't forget about you," she said. "Let's go get you guys some dinner too."

The house definitely had a different feel when she was the only one there. It had been a rare thing for the house to be empty when she was growing up there, and now, since her mother didn't drive, getting the place to herself remained a rare treat. Neither of her parents kept late hours, so their dates usually ended before the evening got late, so being alone there at night was almost unheard of for her. As the evening crept up on her and darkness fell outside, she found herself glad for Petunia's company. The knowledge that she was completely alone on acres of land, surrounded by the Alaskan wilderness, suddenly seemed just a bit ominous to her. True, Malcolm was just a mile down the road, but he had his girls with him, and she didn't want to disturb him. Not for something as silly and unimportant as the fact that she was starting to feel just a tad bit lonely.

She put a movie in and settled down on the soft couch — the thing was almost as old as she was — in the living room. Petunia lay next to her, her head resting on Angie's thigh and her tail lazily thumping against the far armrest. It was cozy. Angie just wished she had some popcorn.

Her eyes were drifting shut by the time the movie ended. She turned the screen off and urged the old dog up. Petunia got up with a groan and a sigh, stretching thoroughly before ambling toward the bedroom.

Angie did one last circuit of the house before following her, cracking the windows open to take advantage of the cooler night air and making sure that the front door was locked. The old house creaked above her, sounding as if it, too, was settling in for bed.

She left the bedroom door open a crack, knowing that the cats would likely want to join her at some point, once they gave up on her parents warming the bed in the master bedroom for them, then slipped beneath the covers, clicking off the bedside light. She felt Petunia jump up on the foot of the bed and curl up into a tight ball. By morning, she knew, the dog would be stretched out beside her.

Feeling comfortable and pleasantly tired, she drifted off to sleep.

Angie awoke a couple of hours later to a low growl coming from somewhere a few inches behind her head. The adrenaline that spiked through her body made her palms prickle and her heart race, but she didn't move so much as a muscle. *Petunia*, she thought as her mind slowly cleared itself of whatever dream she had been having and refocused on the here and now. *It's just Petunia. She must be having a bad dream.*

She rolled over slowly, not wanting to startle the dog out of such an intense sounding dream, and blinked a couple of times as her eyes focused in the dark. What she saw made her pause.

Petunia wasn't passed out on her side, her head on the pillow beside Angie's like she normally was by this point in the night. Instead she was alert, head and ears perked up toward the bedroom door. Angie could see the glint of the dog's open eyes in the light from the bedside clock.

"Petunia?" she whispered. The dog twitched an ear toward her, but kept her attention focused on the door. "Petunia, what—"

She broke off when she heard a long, slow creak come from the floorboards in the hallway. *It's probably one of the cats*, she told herself after a long moment. *Or the house settling.* The fact that her blood felt like ice in her veins told her that she really didn't believe either of those things.

A loud silence hung over the house for moments that seemed to stretch out endlessly, until there was another creak, this one closer and shorter, and a small thud, and Petunia took off from the bed, barking. That split instant was all it took for things to devolve into utter chaos.

This time there was no doubting that what Angie heard were footsteps as someone thudded through the house, away from the barking dog. She practically threw herself out of bed, just barely managing to keep herself from tripping over the sheets, and ran out into the hallway, flipping the light switch to illuminate her way as she did so. The sound of something shattering guided her toward the living room. She was running purely on adrenaline and didn't have even a hint of a plan as she hurried toward the noise.

The living room was dark, and the switch was on the other side of the room. She heard barking and growling, then a shouted curse in a man's voice coming from the direction of the front door. Panicking, Angie went further into the living room, toward the fireplace where the heavy iron poker was kept. She had forgotten about the sound of something shattering, and only made it a couple of steps into the room before her foot came down on something sharp.

She couldn't help the short shriek that burst from her throat as she dropped down to the floor, clutching her foot. From the other side of the room, she heard the front door open and the sound of footsteps thudding across the porch. There was barking too; Petunia's voice was joined by a sudden cacophony from the dog yard.

Blindly, Angie felt her foot and pulled out what felt like a shard of glass. She shuddered as she let it drop to the floor, but forced herself back up and staggered over to the door, which had been left wide open. Flicking the porch light on, she looked out into the small circle that it illuminated. The dogs were still barking from the dog yard, and she could hear Petunia off in the distance, still chasing whoever had been in the house.

"Petunia!" she called. "Pet!"

There was no answering jingle of tags, though the dogs in the yard calmed down slightly at the sound of her voice. Hurt, bleeding, and terrified both for herself and her dog, Angie stumbled back inside, locked the door behind her, and made a beeline for the phone in the kitchen.

5
―――

By the time the police got there, every light in the house was on, and Angie had the fire poker held tightly in her hands. She had never been so relieved at the sight of flashing red and blue lights as the police vehicle turned into the driveway.

She had taken the time to wrap some gauze around her foot in an effort to keep from bleeding all over the house, but she was pretty sure she would need to go get stitches before the night was out. While she wasn't usually squeamish, her stomach threatened to rebel every time she thought about examining the deep wound more closely.

During her wait, she had cracked the front door open a couple of times to call for Petunia, but she hadn't seen or heard anything from the husky, which was another concern that had her stomach tied up in knots. Just how far had Petunia chased the man? Was she lost? Hurt?

Angie bit her lip and closed her eyes, taking a deep breath before opening the door for the police. She watched as the two officers walked up to her door, and hoped that they would be able to find some answers for her.

It took nearly an hour to finish walking them through what had happened that night. She waited in the living room with a cup of tea while they searched the house for other intruders; a concern that hadn't even occurred to her, for which she was grateful. She couldn't imagine how horrible the long wait for the police to arrive would have been if she had been worrying about someone else being in her home.

At last, they returned to the living room. "The house is clear," the elder of the two said. "We looked in every nook and cranny. There's no one else here."

"Thank you," she said, breathing out a sigh of relief.

"We shut all the windows as well, and made sure they were locked."

Angie shivered. It hadn't taken them long to determine how the intruder had gotten in. There was a large gash in the screen of the one of the windows in the living room, which she had opened before going to bed. She wouldn't be making that mistake again; at least if the windows were shut and locked, he would have to break them to get in again, and she would hear that.

"What do I do now?" she asked.

"We've called the incident in and have another car patrolling the area. We'll park in your driveway and keep an eye on the house for the rest of the night. If you need anything, we'll just be a shout away."

"But what about tomorrow? And the night after? There's nothing stopping him from coming back once you're not watching the house anymore."

He sighed, running a hand through his hair. "Without a physical description of the intruder, and without any suspects, there's little we can do. I can recommend a few good security systems for you, which should help put your mind at ease. Motion sensing floodlights and visible security cameras go a long way with discouraging crime. We'll also increase patrols out here for the next week or so. I'm sorry, there's not much more we can do."

She took a deep breath. "It's all right. I understand, I guess."

"Is there someone who can come stay with you until your parents return? It might be safer if you're not here alone."

"Maybe," she said. Malcolm would come stay with her, she knew, once his kids went back to their mother's. In the meantime, maybe Maggie could come stay, but she wasn't sure if she wanted to ask her friend to do that. Maggie had a nine year old son, Joshua, and she didn't want to put him in danger if the burglar did come back.

"You have both of our cards?" the younger one asked. She nodded. "Remember to call us as soon as you know if anything is missing. If we know what he took, we can put an alert out to the local pawn shops. If he tries to sell something he stole, we'll be able to catch him."

"I'll go through the house tomorrow and see if anything is out of place," she said. "I don't think he was here for very long, though. My dog would have woken me up sooner if he was."

The mention of Petunia made her heart clench again. She had mentioned the missing dog to the officers, and they had passed her description along to the other patrol car, with the promise that if anyone spotted her, they would call her immediately. Angie was planning on going out herself at first light to look for the husky.

The officers seemed about ready to wrap up their discussion. They said their goodbyes, promising her once again that they would be parked partway down the driveway, in view of the house, until morning. She opened the front door for them, thanking them genuinely, and followed them out onto the porch. All three of them froze at the sound of a rustling in the bushes in the dark.

"Go back inside," the older of the two said as the younger placed his hand on his sidearm. Angie took a hesitant step backward, then stumbled forward again as a red and white dog stepped into the circle of light.

"Petunia!" she cried out. The dog rushed forward, her entire body wriggling with happiness as Angie petted her. The officers relaxed.

"Looks like you found your dog all right," the younger one said. "They're smart animals. I'm not surprised she found her way back."

"She's the best dog in the world," Angie said, scratching under Petunia's chin. Her fingers came away sticky. "What— is this blood?"

It was.

The younger officer, who seemed to be more of a dog person, crouched down to examine Petunia. "I don't think it's hers. She must have gotten the guy who broke in. We'll take a sample, see if it matches any of the DNA we have on file."

It took another few minutes for them to collect the sample and leave. Angie waited until they were in the squad car before going back inside. She had a feeling she wasn't going to get back to sleep that night. She had a very brave dog to bathe, and then, she thought, she had better take a look at her foot.

6

Angie was exhausted when she went into work that morning. She was running off of only a couple of hours of sleep; whatever she had managed to get before the intruder woke her and Petunia up. She was amazingly grateful to Maggie, who had come over at six to drive her to the doctor's office so they could stitch up the cut in her foot before she headed in to work.

She was so shaken by what had happened the night before that she completely forgot that Malcolm was planning on bringing the girls in for breakfast. She had almost even forgotten what day of the week it was. She did a double take when she saw him walk through the diner's front door with the two excited children. They recognized her and waved happily as he guided them to a booth. He grinned over at her, but the expression faltered when he met her eyes. He raised an eyebrow in a silent question, and she realized that her expression must not have been the cheeriest.

"I'll tell you later," she mouthed, before turning to go grab three waters and a couple of menus for them.

The girls were happy and talkative as she took their orders — they got the pancakes every time, but Malcolm almost always got something different — and she did her best to smile and laugh and act like her usual self. From the concerned look Malcolm was giving her, she got the feeling she wasn't quite managing.

"Here you go!" she said as she brought out their dishes. The pancakes were perfectly made, with chocolate chip and whipped cream smiley faces and sliced strawberries around the edges. Malcolm had ordered a breakfast omelet with hash browns on the side. She had managed to include a bacon smiley face in his omelet, and he grinned at her when he saw it. She smiled back, and this time it felt more genuine.

When she went back to the kitchen, she found a text message on her phone from him. *Are you okay?*

I'll tell you about it later, she replied. *Long story.*

She felt a little bit bad for not telling him about what had happened sooner, but she really hadn't had the time. Maggie had been suitably freaked out, and had offered to stay this coming night at Angie's house with her. Angie declined at first, until Maggie had mentioned that she could make arrangements with her father for Joshua to stay with him. Angie had been all too quick to accept after that. The thought of spending another night alone in that house after what had happened was almost too much to bear.

After Malcolm and his kids left, the rest of her shift seemed to drag by. The lack of sleep was catching up to her, and she was fighting back yawns by the afternoon. It didn't help matters that she already knew she wouldn't be able to sleep very well tonight. She knew that she and Maggie – and probably Petunia as well – would all be on high alert in case the intruder came back. She just wished she knew why they had been there and what they were after. Had it been a random burglary? Or was someone targeting her family for some reason?

Maybe it was due to her tiredness, but paranoia seemed to be dogging her. As her shift neared its end, she could have sworn she felt eyes on her. She paused on her way back to the kitchen with an arm full of dirty plates and looked around the room. She met the eyes of an elderly man who looked familiar. He was staring at her, just a bit too intently. She realized she'd seen him on the day before, at breakfast. He was a regular.

He probably can tell something is wrong, she thought. *He's looking at me because he is concerned, that's all.* She shook herself, trying to remove thoughts of late night intruders from her mind. She didn't want to be any jumpier than her sleep-deprived brain already was.

At long last, her shift ended and she said a quick goodbye to Betty, who had come to cover the evening shift. She stepped out into the parking lot, keys in hand, and looked around for her van. When she didn't see it, she felt a moment of panic until she remembered that Maggie had dropped her off there after the doctor visit. She had completely forgotten that she had made plans with her friend to be picked up at the coffee shop half an hour after her shift ended.

Still feeling discombobulated and out of sorts, she began the short walk through town to the coffee shop, hoping that some caffeine would help perk her up. It could go either way, she knew. It might just make her more jittery, or it might help clear her mind up a bit.

She got up to the counter and ordered a latte, waiting around for a few minutes while they made it. She took it to a small table by the window and sat down, almost collapsing into the chair. She sipped it, but it was too hot to really drink just then, so she put it back down. Resting her arms on the table, she lowered her head to them and closed her eyes. Her foot hurt, her brain felt foggy, and she didn't feel safe in her own home anymore. How had things gone so wrong in just a few hours?

When she picked her head up again, her eyes met someone else's. A pair of watery blue eyes, the same eyes that had been staring at her in the restaurant earlier that day. Mr. Lowery had followed her to the coffee shop.

7

Angie jolted back in her chair, her elbow connecting with the latte. The Styrofoam cup flew off the table and splashed its contents across the floor. Someone gasped, and almost immediately, the barista behind the counter came rushing over with a damp rag. Angie slipped out of her seat to help clean the mess up. When she looked up, Mr. Lowery was walking out the door, his head ducked as he grasped his cup of coffee. He didn't look back.

"Ma'am?"

She turned her attention back to the waitress. "Pardon me?"

"I asked if you were okay. You look pretty shaken."

"Sorry. It's just been a really long day." What else was she supposed to say? 'I think that old man has been following me' might make her sound just a little bit crazy.

"No need to apologize. Would you like another one?"

Angie was about to say yes when she saw Maggie pull up in front of the building. With a sigh, she shook her head. "My ride's here. I had better get going. Thanks so much for helping clean up the mess, and I'm sorry again for spilling coffee over the floor."

She slipped out the front door, still feeling guilty even after the barista's reassurances. She really wasn't herself today.

Maggie greeted her with a cheerful smile, reaching over to push the passenger side door open as Angie neared. "You look like you've been trampled by a moose."

"I feel like I've been trampled by a whole herd of moose. Are you sure you still want to come over tonight? I'm afraid I won't be very good company."

"I happen to like the idea of my best friend not being murdered in her sleep, thank you very much. There's no way I'm letting you stay at that house alone until they catch the guy who broke in."

Angie grinned, reaching over to roll down the window as Maggie pulled out onto the street. "I feel like I should protest, but honestly, I'm just really glad I'll have company tonight."

Maggie was in a good mood, and it was infectious. Angie found herself singing along to songs on the radio with her friend as they headed back out of town toward the house. They paused at the mailbox at the end of the long driveway to grab the day's mail, then drove the rest of the way up toward the house.

Before going in, Angie and Maggie walked around the house to make sure that no windows had been broken and that the doors were all still locked. She had been worried that the intruder might come back while she was at work earlier that day, but unless they had somehow managed to break in without leaving a scratch on the place, she was pretty sure that they hadn't.

Inside, Petunia greeted them at the door. Angie made a beeline for the kitchen to give the dog a couple of extra treats. She was still proud of the husky for defending her the night before. She hated to think what might have happened to her if the dog hadn't been there. Would she have even woken up when the intruder got to her room? For all she knew, without Petunia, he might have killed her in her sleep. She very well might owe her life to the dog.

She tossed the mail on the kitchen table then put her mud boots on and walked outside to take care of her father's dogs. Maggie followed behind her, chatting happily and occasionally handing Angie a dish as she changed out the water. When they were done, they went inside and sat at the kitchen table. Angie propped her foot up on the chair across from her as she sorted through the mail.

"Bills, bills, junk mail… wait, this is weird." She pulled out a folded up piece of paper from the pile. It wasn't in an envelope, and it didn't have their address on it. All it had was her last name, scribbled across the folded paper in a messy scrawl. *Seaver*.

"What is it?" Maggie asked.

"I don't know," Angie said. She unfolded the paper and read it slowly, icy fear beginning to creep through her veins with the very first word.

Leave the watch in your mailbox tonight or I'll come back, and this time I'll be waiting with a knife when you wake up.

It was written hastily, the words slashing across the page with enough force to tear the paper in a couple of areas. Her hands shaking, Angie put it down on the table. Maggie grabbed it, reading it quickly.

"The watch? What watch? Angie, what's going on?"

"They must be talking about an old watch my father found while he was out with the dogs," she replied. "I don't understand, though… is that really what this is all about?"

Now that she thought about it, she realized that all of her problems hadn't started until her father brought the watch home. Still, it didn't make any sense to her. Why would someone care so much about an old watch? And who even knew that her father had found it? She hadn't told anyone other than Malcolm and Betty. She didn't think her father had time to tell anyone about it before he left, either.

No, there was one more person who knew. Whoever Malcolm had taken the watch to be cleaned. But it didn't make sense that this would be that person. They had the watch already, so there would be no reason for them to send a threat like this.

"This is a serious threat, Angie. We have to call my dad."

Maggie's father was Detective O'Brien, who Angie knew as a good man and a better cop. She knew her friend was right. This wasn't something she could deal with on her own.

"Okay," she said. "I'll make the call. I'm glad you're here, Mags. It's always better to have company when a crazy person is sending you death threats."

She and her friend shared a weak smile, then Angie stood up and grabbed the landline phone.

Half an hour later, a police cruiser pulled up into the driveway. Angie and Maggie had made coffee while they waited, and had left the note where it was, realizing belatedly that the police might be able to lift fingerprints from the paper.

She let Detective O'Brien into the house and thanked him for coming all the way out there.

"It's my job," he pointed out. "Plus, any friend of Maggie's is a friend of mine too. You practically grew up at my place during the summer back when you were kids, Angie. I can't say I'm thrilled that my daughter is involved in all of this now, but I can promise you that nothing in the world could drag me away from this case."

They showed him the note first. He pulled on latex gloves and read the paper carefully before tucking it into an evidence bag.

"I'll take this back to the station," he said. "Now, tell me more about this watch."

Angie did, telling him everything she could remember about how her father had found it, and describing the watch in as much detail as she could.

"Where is it now?"

"Malcolm took it to get cleaned," she told him. "I'm

not sure who he took it to. I can see if he can get it back as soon as possible."

"Please do. We'll probably want to take the watch in as evidence as well. Figure out what this is all about if we can. It's possible that it could be connected to a crime. I'll dig through some of the cold cases and see if there's anything about a stolen or missing watch."

"What's Angie supposed to do in the meantime, Dad?" Maggie asked.

He ran his hand through his hair, lips pursed as he thought. "I'll post someone outside of the house for the next couple of nights. We don't have enough men to do it long term, though. Is there someone who could come stay with you until your parents get back? Normally I'd suggest someone in your position get out of town, but I understand with the dogs, that's hard to do."

"Malcolm can probably stay with me starting tomorrow night," Angie said. "I can make up the guest bed for him. He's got his kids for the weekend, but they will be going back home tomorrow evening."

"And I'll stay here tonight," Maggie said. She and her father exchanged glares for a long moment, until the older man gave a sigh of defeat.

"It's your choice, Maggie. Just be careful. I've got to get going now; I left Joshua with some of the guys at the station. I didn't tell him that I was responding to a call made by his mother. Didn't want the poor kid to worry too much. Keep the doors and windows locked. I'll have a squad car out here within the hour. They'll be parked right outside of the house. If you need anything, shout for them or flicker the porch light on and off a few times. I'll give you their cell phone number too, but you know as well as I do how spotty the cell phone service can be out here."

Angie thanked him and waited as he and his daughter said their goodbyes to each other. He walked to his car and got in, shooting a worried glance behind him. She and Maggie waved as he drove away.

8

Even with the squad car parked outside, neither of them got much sleep that night. Earlier in the evening it was easier to relax and joke around a bit, almost treating the whole thing as a big adventure, but as darkness fell outside, it got harder and harder to keep the conversation light.

Angie was impressed with her friend's loyalty. With every creak and groan of the house, every sound that came from outside, the two of them would jump, then laugh nervously, but never once did Maggie seem to regret her choice to stay over.

They were in the middle of making breakfast the

next morning after a long, uneventful night when Angie's phone rang and her father's name came up on the caller ID. She stared at it for a moment, her stomach suddenly twisting. She still hadn't told him everything that had happened. She wasn't sure she wanted to. Not yet, anyway. Not while he and her mother were out of town and unable to do anything anyway.

She put down the knife she was using to dice onions for the omelets and answered the phone.

"Hey, Dad," she said. "How is everything going?"

"Hey, Angie. Things are going pretty well. The doctors think they will be able to help your mother, at least with some of the shaking she has. How is everything there? Have the dogs been able to get out for any exercise?"

"I took them out to the big yard the day before

yesterday," she said. "I didn't have time yesterday, unfortunately."

"Busy day at the diner?"

She hesitated. "Yeah, something like that. Anyway, all the animals are doing fine. The cats have been stuck to me like glue. I think they miss you and Mom."

He chuckled. "Probably mostly your mother. She babies those two like nothing else. How are you doing? It's not too much for you, is it?"

"No," she said. "I've got everything under control here. When will you guys be back?"

"We're looking at Thursday evening now."

"Okay."

"I hope you aren't too lonely there. I know how quiet the house can be."

"Maggie spent the night with me last night, and I'm sure Malcolm will keep me company this week. Plus, I've got about twenty dogs here. I think it would be impossible to be lonely."

They both chuckled and said their goodbyes. Angie hung up the phone and turned to see Maggie looking at her.

"You really aren't going to tell him?"

"I'll tell him when he gets back," Angie said with a shrug, feeling somewhat defensive. "I don't want to worry him, not while he and my mom are down there trying to figure things out. He wouldn't be able to do anything about it anyway, and it would just make the trip worse for them."

"You know he's friends with my father," Maggie said. "What if my dad tells them?"

Angie bit her lip. She hadn't thought of that. "Well, I'm sticking to my choice. I can't control what your father tells mine, but I think that I'm making the right decision."

For a moment, Maggie looked like she was about to say something else, but then she shrugged. "It's your choice. Now, let's finish those omelets. I'm starving."

Maggie left at noon to go get Joshua from her father's house and spend the rest of the day with him, leaving Angie alone at the house. She decided to take some time outside with the dogs and let them run around in the big yard with the kiddie pools full of water. She figured if she was going to be safe anywhere on the property, it would be surrounded by a pack of her father's huskies.

It was a nice day; a bit too nice, in fact. She was already sweating by the time the kiddie pools were filled with water and the dogs had been moved over to the large area. Thankfully there were a couple of folding chairs set up in the shade and she sat down on one, dragging a pool over and sticking her foot in the water while she watched the dogs run around. Petunia darted around with the pack for a few minutes before coming to lay in the shade next to Angie. Angie closed her eyes, leaning her head back and letting herself relax. If she didn't have the weight of that threatening note hanging over her head, this would have been the perfect day.

She called Malcolm a few hours later, when she knew that he would be about to leave for Anchorage, and let him know everything that had happened. She felt a bit guilty when he told her that she should have called him earlier.

"I just didn't want to make you worry while you were with the kids," she said, her reasoning similar to why she hadn't told her father. "I know there's nothing you'd be able to do about it, and it would just upset you. I'm fine, I've been hanging out with the dogs all day, and Maggie spent the night last night. I was wondering if you could come over this evening, though. Detective O'Brien doesn't think I should be here on my own, even with the police outside."

"Of course," he said. "I'll pick up food on my way back, and we can watch a movie or something. You really think all this links back to the watch?"

"It has to," she said. "It's the only thing that makes sense, after that note."

"Who even knows you have it?"

"You. Betty. My dad. Whoever you gave the watch to

clean. That's it. I can't think of anyone else, other than my mom, I guess."

"Well, I'll pick it up from the guy on my way down to Anchorage with the kids and bring it back so you can give it to the police. Are you sure you'll be all right for the next two hours? You could come with us."

"I'll be fine," Angie said. "If I'm being honest, I don't really want to leave the house. As long as I'm here, I know that no one is getting inside. If I go away, someone could very well sneak in and hide somewhere and I would never even know it until it's too late. No, I'm good to hold down the fort here. Thanks for coming over tonight though, Malcolm."

"Of course. We'll brainstorm this evening and see if we can figure something out."

The hours seemed to drag by. A sense of unease

hung over Angie all day. After she put the dogs back in their yard, each of them tethered to their spot, she went indoors with Petunia and double checked that all the windows were shut and locked before she walked around the house, randomly checking in closets and under beds. She hated feeling this way. She hated feeling so paranoid. She wasn't usually a jumpy person, but the fact remained that someone had already managed to get into her house once and for all she knew had been moments away from murdering her. Something like that tended to get on one's nerves. She thought she was handling it pretty well, all things considered. Still, she felt a deep sense of relief when Malcolm called her later that evening and told her he was about half an hour away, and he had Chinese food in the car with him.

When he got there Angie let the police, who were parked outside her home, know that he was cleared to get through. The officers politely turned down her offer of some noodles and eggrolls, and she told them to come up to the house if they changed their mind..

She shut the door behind Malcolm as he made his way to the kitchen, where he put the bags of food down on the table and began going through the cupboards to get out the plates, forks, and glasses for their meal. She helped him get everything ready, and the two of them sat down before facing the elephant in the room.

"I take it nothing eventful happened between when we talked and now?" he said.

She shook her head. "Nope. It was as quiet as could be."

"That's good."

She nodded, then shrugged. "I almost wish he would have tried to come back. That way, the police would've been able to bring him in and all of this would be over."

"He's probably smart enough not to try to break in with the police right outside," Malcolm pointed out. "I'm really worried about you, Angie. You are in danger. Are you sure you don't want to just go to a hotel or something?"

"I can't," she said. "I've got to stay here and take care of the animals."

"You could hire a pet sitter."

She shook her head. "I thought about that," she admitted. "But I don't think I could live with myself if I did hire someone to look after them and they ended up getting hurt. This is my problem. I'm not putting someone else in danger. I feel guilty enough just asking you and Maggie to spend time with me."

"There is no way I'm leaving you here alone after everything that happened. That is still happening,"

Malcolm said. "You don't have to feel guilty about that. It's my choice."

"I really appreciate it," she said, giving him a small smile. "Oh, did you get the watch back?"

"I did. Here." He reached into his pocket and pulled out a small cloth bag, sliding it across the table to Angie. She picked it up and opened it, taking out a shiny gold wristwatch that was almost unrecognizable. Turning it over, she admired it gently. "Wow, it really is a beautiful piece. It must be pretty expensive." She turned it around to the back and squinted at the inscription. It had been cleaned up a bit and was a lot easier to read. She could make two names and a date.

Andy Wilson and Charlese Wilson June 6, 1955

"At least we know who it belonged to now," she said, turning it back over and gently placing the watch back into the bag. "I wonder if it was an anniversary gift or something."

"We should search the names," Malcolm suggested. "See if we can find out anything about them. It would be neat to be able to return the watch to its rightful owner."

"That would be amazing," she said, then sighed. "But with everything going on, I should probably just turn it over to the police like we planned."

"You're right," he said somberly. "Sorry."

"Not your fault," she said with a sigh. "My dad's going to be disappointed."

"I think he'd be a lot more than disappointed if you ended up getting hurt over a silly watch," he said, reaching across the table to take her hand. She smiled at him and squeezed his fingers.

"You're right. Come on, let's eat. I'll take the watch to Detective O'Brien tomorrow after work. In the meantime, let's try to forget about all of this and just enjoy the evening together. I made up the guest bed for you, put fresh sheets on it and everything. Thanks for staying here, Malcolm."

9

Angie was dead on her feet the next morning, barely managing to take care of the dogs and stumble out of the house on time in order to open the diner. She and Malcolm had stayed up late the night before, watching movies and talking about what they wanted to do over the summer before falling asleep on the couch. She had woken up around three in the morning, her neck crooked awkwardly against the side of the couch, and stumbled into her room to get a few hours of comfortable sleep after covering Malcolm's sleeping form with a blanket. The night had been uneventful, thankfully. She found herself hoping that maybe the person who had broken in and who had left the note had given up, though she knew that wasn't very likely. She hoped that with the watch in evidence, Detective O'Brien might be able to begin making sense of the case. She had it with her, tucked away inside her purse, and was planning on stopping at the police station after her shift at the diner.

Grace was working with her that morning. Angie was glad for the company; Grace always seemed to be in a good mood and was easy to chat with. Angie didn't mention her problems with the mysterious home intruder, but she did tell her about her parents being out of town to visit some new doctors and all the time she had been enjoying with Maggie and Malcolm.

It was Monday, so after the early rush of people stopping in on their way to work to grab a coffee or a quick, greasy breakfast, the morning was pretty slow. Grace and Angie took turns bussing tables, so that Angie wouldn't have to spend all of her time waiting for an order to come into the kitchen. It was Angie's turn to go out and take the order when the bell rang at about ten-thirty. She made sure her apron was straight and grabbed a hot pot of coffee and a clean mug before pushing her way through the door that led to the dining area. She paused halfway through the doorway, her eyes landing on Mr. Lowery. Her skin prickled, remembering the way he had been watching her the other day and how he had followed her to the coffee shop. He wasn't paying any attention to her now, and she wondered if maybe she just imagined the strangeness of the other day. She started toward him, only to freeze again when she realized something, something that had somehow escaped her memory before.

Mr. Lowery had been sitting close enough to her and Betty when she told Betty about the watch, and would have easily overheard their conversation. She stumbled, and the mug she was holding slipped out of her grasp, shattering on the floor. Mr. Lowery looked over at her, and she quickly dropped to her knees, scooping the shattered shards into her apron. She heard footsteps approaching and looked up, but it was just Grace, coming over to help.

"Are you okay?" the younger woman asked.

"I'm fine," Angie said. "It just slipped out of my hand."

"Here, I'll clean this up. It's okay."

Reluctantly, she left Grace to clean up the last shards of the broken mug and hurried back to the kitchen to grab another coffee cup. Mr. Lowery didn't even look up as she approached him until she was standing right by his shoulder.

"Just the usual, thanks," he said.

"Sure thing," she replied weakly.

She'd been hoping that Grace would be the one to take the order out, but the younger woman was busy helping out another table by the time Mr. Lowery's food was ready. She took a deep breath, telling herself once again that she was just being paranoid

— there was no way old Mr. Lowery was the one who had broken into her home — then stepped out of the kitchen toward the older man. She was beginning to relax. He hadn't so much as glanced her way once through the window in the kitchen. He certainly wasn't acting as though he had recently left a death threat in her mailbox. *He's older than my dad,* she thought as she walked toward him. *He probably isn't spry enough to climb through a window even if he wanted to. It couldn't have been him.*

"Here you go," she said, setting the plate down in front of him. He nodded and grunted his thanks as he reached for his fork. As he did so, his sleeve rode up, exposing a bandage around his wrist. Angie stared at it. He must have noticed something in her change of posture, because he glanced up at her, then down at his arm. "Got a nasty cut from a table saw," he said, tugging his sleeve back down. "Could've been a lot worse. I got lucky."

Angie nodded, smiled, muttered something encouraging, and turned to hurry back to the kitchen.

"I'm overthinking things," she muttered to herself as she shut the door behind her. But still, she couldn't get the memory of the sticky blood under Petunia's chin out of her mind. Whoever had broken in must be walking around with an injury right this moment, and she couldn't figure out whether Mr. Lowery's mysterious wound was just a coincidence, or in fact evidence of his guilt. She made a mental note to mention it to Detective O'Brien, and tried to focus on her job in the kitchen. The food wouldn't make itself, after all, and she had two orders waiting to be fulfilled. The next time she went out, Mr. Lowery was gone, and there was a five dollar tip waiting for her under his plate.

She went directly to the police station after her shift ended. She was relieved when the woman working reception — not Maggie; she was working different hours for the summer and Angie still hadn't gotten used to them — told her Detective O'Brien was there, and he came out to see her almost immediately. His concern for her was evident as they walked back to his office together.

"Has anything happened? I wasn't expecting a visit today."

"I just came here to give you the old watch my father found," she said, pulling it out of her purse and handing it over to him. "I thought you might want to see it."

"Thank you," he said, taking it out and carefully looking it over. "With any luck, this will be the key in solving this case. Unfortunately, I'm not sure how quickly we will be able to get it back to you, not while it's evidence in an active case."

"Don't worry about it," she said. "Trust me when I say that the priority is figuring all of this out as quickly as possible. I don't care if the watch is stuck in evidence for years, as long as I can sleep easily at night again."

"We'll do what we can," he promised. "Do you have someone staying with you at the house today?"

"Malcolm is coming over again," she told him. "I think we're planning on going out and spending some time with the dogs. He's going to run a few with his team on the quad."

"That sounds like a good way to spend the afternoon. I'm sure being active on the property will help keep any potential intruders away. I've got a squad car keeping an eye on your house right now, to make sure no one tries to break in while you're gone, but they have instructions to leave once you get home. We just don't have the men to keep the watch up indefinitely."

"It'll be okay," she said. "Now that I'm aware of the danger and have someone staying with me, I think I'll be a lot safer. I won't do anything stupid, and I won't go anywhere alone around the property."

"I know. You're smart girl, Angie. Take care."

She thanked him again and left the police station, glancing over to the front desk out of habit before remembering that Maggie was off today. She considered seeing if her friend wanted to go out for coffee, then decided against it. She didn't want to spend too long in town; Malcolm was supposed to meet her at her house in about an hour. She didn't want to get there late, but she also didn't want to get there before he got there, since the police were supposed to leave when she arrived and she wasn't sure she wanted to be at home alone right now.

After a few moments of indecision, she decided to head to the library. The internet in town was a lot faster than what her parents had at their house, and she wanted to look up those names on the back of the watch.

The Lost Bay Library was a small, old building that hadn't changed one iota since Angie had been a child. She made her way over to computers that looked as if they had been there since her high school years and logged in to a guest account. She still needed to get a library card. She still needed to do a lot of things to make the move feel more permanent.

Thanks to the inscription on the watch, she had two names and a date to search. The web browser digested her request for a few long moments before coming up with a surprisingly long list of articles from the local newspaper. She clicked the earliest dated link and was brought to a page that looked like it had been scanned in from an old newspaper. It was a wedding announcement, and the names and date matched the inscription on the watch, other than the fact that Charlese was mentioned by her maiden name; McCray.

After reading through the short article, she went back to the search page and clicked on the next link. The title of this article sent a chill of foreboding through her. *Man Goes Missing During Camping Trip With Wife.* The story went on to tell the story of the

Wilson couple, who had been married only two years at this point, and a summer camping trip with friends gone wrong.

According to the article, Andy had gone fishing at Lime Lake the morning of the second day and had never come back. His pole and tackle box had been found by the lake, but there was no sign of him. The search had lasted three days; they had even called in a search and rescue dog team with no luck. Angie read through the story quickly, her heart beating quickly, then paged back to click on through to further articles. Another search party was sent out a few weeks later, this time looking for a body, but they hadn't found anything either. Six months later, Andy Wilson was officially declared dead, but despite the funeral that had been held for him, no body had ever been found. It was as though he had simply vanished.

Maybe my dad found more than a lost heirloom when he found that watch, she thought. *Maybe he found the location of Andy Wilson's body.*

10

Angie printed out copies of the articles to show to Malcolm, then logged out of the computer and packed her things up, pausing momentarily to browse the shelves before she left the library. She really did need to get a library card, but she didn't have time to do it now or she would be late to meet Malcolm.

She was distracted as she walked out the door, and didn't even see the small child until she bumped into him. Only a reflexive grab at the boy's shoulder kept him on his feet, and she apologized profusely as she realized she had almost trampled a kid.

"Are you okay?" she asked, crouching down to his level. She recognized the boy, but it took her a moment to place him. It wasn't until he spoke that she remembered the sticky hands reaching for her plate.

"Yeah," he said, rubbing at his shoulder. "Sorry for running."

"It's okay. I should have been looking where I was going." She straightened up and looked around. "Where are your parents?" Surely the kid was too young to be here on his own.

"I'm here with my gramma," he said, pointing at an old powder blue car. Angie recognized the elderly woman as someone who stopped in semi-regularly at the diner. She was carrying a pile of books, and a few dropped off the top.

"Here, let me help with that," Angie said, hurrying

forward to pick them up off the ground. Mikey trailed along behind her.

"Oh, thanks," the woman said. "I probably should have done this in two trips."

"It's no problem at all. Here, give me half your stack." She took the books from the woman and turned back toward the library.

"Mikey, get the door."

The boy obliged, and Angie thanked him as she walked back into the library. She and the woman dropped the books off in the return bin inside.

"Whew, thank you. My son was supposed to help me with this today, but he's been caught up in a project of his lately. I'm afraid I didn't catch your name the other day. You work at the diner, don't you?"

"That's right. I'm Angie Seaver."

"It's nice to meet you. I've known your father since he was a young lad. He's a good man. I'm Delphi McCray. And this is my grandson, Mikey, whom you've already met."

"I sure have," Angie said with a grin, as she first shook Delphi's hand, then Mikey's. "I'm sure I'll see you both around. I've got to get going now, but I'm glad I could help."

They shared a polite goodbye, then Angie went out to the parking lot and got into her car, checking her watch. She was going to be a few minutes late, but it couldn't be helped. Doing a good deed was more important than being on time. Malcolm would understand. She just hoped that the police let him by without her there.

Malcolm was already at her house when she got there, and was leaning against the police cruiser chatting with the occupants. She waved as she pulled up, and all three men waved back. Once she was parked she walked over to join them them, shading her eyes against the sun.

"This young man told us he had permission to be here, but we wanted to make sure you knew him before we left," the officer in the passenger seat said as she approached.

"Yep, Malcolm's the one staying with me for now. Thanks for double checking, though. Sorry I'm late, I got held up at the library after work. I know you guys were waiting for me to get here before you left."

"Not a problem, ma'am. We'll get going now, though. We've been parked out front since this morning, and haven't seen hide nor hair of another human being until Mr. Miles here arrived. The dogs have all been quiet, and we just finished a quick check of the exterior of the house. You're good to go."

"Thank you. I really appreciate it."

She and Malcolm stepped back as the cruiser pulled away, watching as it kicked up dust on its way down the long driveway. Once it was out of sight, she turned to him and spoke.

"Sorry for being late. I hope they didn't give you too much trouble."

"Not at all. They were perfectly nice and we had a chat about dogs while we were waiting. I'm glad they didn't just take my word that I was supposed to be here."

"Me too," she said, chuckling. "I think Detective O'Brien would have been pretty upset with them if they did that. We're on our own now, though. I stopped in at the police station after work to hand over that watch, and he told me they don't have enough men to keep someone posted here for any longer."

"We'll be fine," he said, throwing an arm around her shoulders as they walked toward the house. "With the two of us and the dogs, the intruder would have to either be very stupid or very determined to try to break in again."

"They might be pretty determined, if my theory is right," she said. She dug through her purse for her keys and unlocked the front door, stepping back to let Malcolm go first. "I did some research at the library, and I'm pretty sure that Andy Wilson is dead."

Malcolm read through the articles she printed out while Angie greeted Petunia and the cats and made sure the house was locked up tight. Once she was finished, she poured them both glasses of cool water and sat at the table across from him.

"Wow," he said with a low whistle when he was done. "That poor couple. Only married two years before Andy up and vanished. And it sounds like she never got any sort of closure. Do you think his body might be somewhere near where your father found the watch?"

"I think it's more than likely," she said grimly. "The thing is, my dad told me what park he was at when he found the watch and there's no lake anywhere near there. The article said he was fishing at a lake when he vanished. I'm not sure what to make of that."

"Lime Lake," he muttered. "I think I know where that is. There's a map of the area hanging in the barn; let's go look at that."

They got up and relocated to the barn with Petunia following eagerly behind them. Inside the building, Malcolm led the way over to one of the cluttered walls and he and Angie leaned forward, squinting at a yellowing map of the town and the surrounding areas.

"Here's Lime Lake," Malcolm said, pointing to a small lake to the northwest of town. "I knew it sounded familiar. I've gone there before, when your dad was first teaching me how to handle a team of sled dogs. The trails there are nice and wide, and in the winter the lake freezes completely over."

"This doesn't make any sense. The park he was at the day he found the watch is all the way over here," she said, pointing to a small area directly to the east of town. "Why would Andy's watch be all the way over there if he disappeared at Lime Lake? Maybe I'm wrong about all of this and he lost the watch sometime before he vanished."

"I don't know," Malcolm said, frowning at the map. "They searched the area with dogs, according to the article, and didn't find anything. If his body wasn't there, it would explain why they had no luck. If they were searching the Lime Lake area —" He drew a circle around the lake with his finger. "And the body was over here –" He circled the park that Angie had pointed out.. "Then that would explain why they couldn't find anything. Maybe someone killed him and hid his body far enough away that they knew the search parties wouldn't stumble across it."

"That means someone would've had to have found him while he was out camping, killed him, dragged his body back to a car, and then stashed it in the park over here, all with no one noticing."

"It's too bad the article didn't mention who the couple went camping with," Malcolm said, frowning at the old map. "Maybe one of their friends killed him. Or maybe the wife did it. Is she still alive?"

"I'm not sure. I didn't think to check," Angie admitted.

"I—" Malcolm was interrupted by a cacophony of barking. Petunia, who had been sniffing around the fridge where the meat was stored for the dogs, perked her ears up then took off through the open door, adding her voice to the fray. The two of them exchanged a look then dashed out after her, heading toward the dog yard.

The yard was in chaos. All of Angie's father's dogs were tugging at the ends of their tethers as they barked at the three intruders at the fence line.

"Blake! Aspen! Thor! What are you doing here?"

Malcolm raced toward the three loose huskies and Angie followed. She recognized the three as dogs that Malcolm had inherited from a friend of her father's who had passed away a few months ago. The big, dark husky — she wasn't sure which one it was — was circling around Petunia with his hackles up. Petunia was standing stiff-legged, a low growl coming from her throat. The other huskies looked younger, and were busy barking at the dogs in the dog yard.

Most huskies got along with other dogs pretty well. They had to, if they were expected to run in a team and pass other teams on the trail without races devolving into a mess of dog fights. Still, three strange dogs arriving on territory that Angie's pack considered their own was a recipe for trouble. She hurried forward to grab Petunia's collar before the stand off could result in a fight. Malcolm grabbed the big black husky by his collar, then looked around helplessly.

"I need a leash or something!"

"Here, put him in the barn. I'll put Petunia away and grab some leashes from indoors."

She dropped the red and white husky off inside and grabbed a couple of leashes from the closet by the front door, then ran back outside to help Malcolm wrangle his dogs.

11

"How on earth did they get out?" Angie asked, frowning at the three huskies, all of which looked very proud of themselves. Two were in the cab of Angie's van, and one was in the back of Malcolm's car.

"I don't know. When I first saw them, I thought they must have slipped their collars somehow, but they all still have their collars on. Maybe some animal wandered too close to my yard and they broke their tethers trying to chase it, but all of the equipment I have is only a few months old. It shouldn't be possible for them to be loose. We'd better hurry, I want to check on the other dogs and make sure none of them are running loose."

"All right. I'll follow you over."

She got into the van, absently shoving one of the panting dogs into the back when he tried to crawl up front. "Sorry, you're both too big to be lap dogs. Settle down."

At least the dogs are happy, she thought as she pulled out of the driveway after Malcolm. They definitely seemed to have enjoyed their bid for freedom. She was glad they had made their way over to her property instead of taking off into the great Alaskan wilderness that the property bordered. She knew he was worried about his other dogs. If more of them had gotten loose, somehow, then there was no telling where they could be. Huskies were bred for running, and they could go for miles before tiring. Of course, in this heat, they would probably find a shady creek to play in before going too far.

Two more dogs were wandering loose in Malcolm's yard when they pulled in. She helped him corral them — the bag of dog treats she found in the van's center console helped — before putting all five of the dogs away.

"I don't understand," he said as they hooked the dogs back up. "How did they get loose? Nothing's broken. They're all still wearing their collars. Dewey and Raptor are still missing, but they others are all still tied up."

"Maybe someone came by and tried to steal them," Angie suggested, frowning. "The gate was left open, and I don't think the dogs could do that."

"I've got to go look for them," he said, running a hand through his hair. "Do you think I should call the police?"

"I can call them for you, if you want," she said. "If

you want to head out and look for them, I'll head home and call the police and keep an eye on the property. It's possible the missing two might show up there, like the others did."

"Are you sure? I don't want to leave you alone."

"I'm sure," she said. "We've got to find the dogs. It doesn't make any sense for us both to go out together, not when the dogs could be anywhere. And I don't want to leave the house alone for too long. I'm going to feel a lot better if I'm there, holding down the fort, than if the house is sitting empty for who knows how long. Anyone could come by and break in."

"Angie..."

"It will be fine," she said firmly. "The dogs matter right now. The sooner we find them the better."

"Will you do me a favor and at least bring another dog into the house with you? I'll feel better if I know you've got a couple of dogs indoors to watch your back."

"I'll bring Oracle in," she promised, stepping closer to kiss his cheek. "Now, go find those missing dogs. I'll go home and call Detective O'Brien and let him know what happened. The dogs couldn't have let themselves loose like this. Someone must have done this to them, and the sooner the police know about it, the better."

"Shoot. I just realized that if someone did let the dogs go, they could have stolen Dewey and Raptor. If I text you pictures of them, can you email them to the detective? That way the police can be on the lookout for them in case someone tries to sell them or someone gets spotted with them."

"Of course," she said, feeling sick to her stomach at

the thought of the dogs being stolen. "Good luck, Malcolm. I hope you find them."

She drove back home alone, her mind on the missing dogs. She knew her father had had issues with well-meaning activists interfering with his dogs in the past, which was why he had a padlock on the gate to the dog yard. It was an unfortunate fact of life for anyone who owned sled dogs. The media had had the sport in its sights for a while now, and not everyone agreed with the practice of dog sled racing, or with keeping dogs outside. Angie would never understand the people who thought releasing or stealing working dogs was a solution to anything. The vast Alaskan wilderness held innumerable dangers for dogs, and a lost dog would have a tough time surviving out there.

She parked the vehicle close to the porch and hurried inside, making the call to the police station right away. She was notified that Detective O'Brien had already left for the day, but was assured that all of the officers would be notified of the missing dogs. She was given an email address to send the photos to. After hanging up, and while her laptop connected to the sluggish internet, she went out to the dog yard to bring Oracle in.

The young, energetic black and white husky was only too happy to go with her back to the house. Just inside the front door she made him sit down and held his face so he was looking her in the eyes.

"Oracle, you're only here to help protect me in case someone breaks in. You are not here to dig through the trash. And you are definitely not here to chase the cats. Am I clear? Do not chase the cats."

She gave him her best stern look, then unclasped his leash. He took off like a whirlwind, greeting Petunia in a flurry of wagging tails and then darting around, sniffing every inch of the house he was so rarely invited into. She winced as he ran into an end table, nearly knocking a lamp over.

There was a reason the young, energetic dogs usually lived outside.

"Come on," she muttered, looking out the window. "Where are you, dogs?"

As if on cue, she heard more barking from the dog yard. She jolted and reached for the door handle, before jerking her hand back as if stung. The dogs weren't barking at Malcolm's missing huskies. They were barking at the powder blue sedan that was coming down her driveway.

12

She watched as the car pulled to a stop behind her, peering out from behind the curtain in the living room window. Her mind raced. Had this all been a setup? Had someone purposely released Malcolm's dogs in order to lure him away and get her on her own? *There's no way they could have known I wouldn't go with him to look for the dogs*, she thought. Maybe they just wanted the house empty, so they could search it in peace. She hadn't told anyone other than Malcolm that she was giving the watch to the police. Whoever was looking for it probably thought she still had it.

Her frown deepened when she saw Delphi get out of

the driver's seat, but something inside of her relaxed. The elderly woman was hardly a threat. She stepped back from the window and opened the door.

"Hello," she called out. Delphi waved at her, but didn't smile. Her eyes scanned the yard; she seemed nervous at the sound of the barking dogs from the back.

Angie heard thundering footsteps behind her and reached down just in time to grab Oracle before he darted out the door. "He's friendly," she called out as she struggled to hold on to him, "but he's a bit hyper. I'm going to go put him in the other room."

She dragged the husky to the closest room with a door on it — the bathroom — and shut him inside. When she got back to the front door, the elderly woman was standing on the porch, staring nervously at Petunia, who had wandered out to greet her.

"She won't bite, will she?"

"No. She's very gentle, unlike Oracle. He's nice, but he's a wrecking ball. Why don't you come in?"

She stepped back, holding the door as Delphi and Petunia both came into the house. She shut it behind them, then turned to face the older woman.

"Sorry, you're probably wondering why I'm here," Delphi said. She looked around with mild interest, still shooting occasional wary glances at the dog. *Not a dog person,* Angie thought.

"Not to sound rude, but I am. How do you even know where I live?"

"It's a small town, dear. Everyone knows where you live."

Maybe it was just the circumstances, but the words gave Angie chills. She shook herself, hoping that the other woman didn't notice her discomfort.

"Well, what can I help you with?"

"That's a bit complicated, I'm afraid. Oh dear, she must smell the snacks I carry around for my grandson." Delphi lifted her purse out of Petunia's curious nose, and Angie gently shooed the dog away.

She opened her mouth, wanting to get the conversation back on track, but the landline started ringing before she could say anything. She hesitated, then gestured toward the living room. "Go ahead and sit down. I've got to see who that is. Someone let my boyfriend's dogs out of his yard and we're still looking for two of them, so it might be important. I'll be right back."

She walked slowly toward the kitchen, feeling

uneasy about the whole thing. Too many coincidences had happened that day, but she just couldn't see how they all fit together. She knew that letting Delphi in might have been a mistake, given everything that had been happening, but she just couldn't see how a little old lady could be dangerous.

"Hello?" she said, picking up the phone.

"Hey, it's me," Malcolm said. "I got a call about the dogs. Someone found them about five miles away from here. I'm going to pick them up now."

"Thank goodness," she breathed. "That's good news."

The kitchen door creaked open behind her and she turned around to see Delphi peeking in at her.

"Can I have a glass of water?" she asked in a stage whisper.

"Hold on a second," she said into the phone. Malcolm, who had been saying something about the dogs, paused. "Of course," she said to Delphi. "Do you want ice?"

She nodded. Angie reached into the cupboard to get a glass.

"Is someone there?" Malcolm asked.

"Yeah. This woman I met at the diner, and then again at the library showed up here a few minutes ago. Delphi McCray. She knows my dad, I guess." She put a couple ice cubes in the glass, then ran the cold water from the sink.

"Wait, did you say McCray?"

"Yeah, why?"

"That was Charlese Wilsons's maiden name," he told her. "Is she related to the missing man's wife?"

Angie handed the glass over to the woman, who took it and left the kitchen. Angie frowned, but waited until she was out of earshot before responding.

"She must be. I didn't make the connection before, even though I had just read the articles before I ran into her. That must be why she's here."

"Could she be the one behind all of this?" he asked, sounding worried.

"I don't think so." She lowered her voice, glancing

toward the kitchen door. "She's old, Malcolm. There's no way she could have broken into my house. And I'm pretty sure whoever did was a man, anyway."

"Still... be careful Angie. Do you want me to come there?"

"No, go get your dogs," she told him. "She probably just wants to talk about the watch. I don't think I have anything to worry about. I'm pretty sure I could pick her up without breaking a sweat. She's tiny."

"All right," he said after a moment. She could tell by his tone that he was unsure. "I'll hurry. Be safe, Angie."

"I will be," she promised.

They said their goodbyes and Angie put the phone

back in its cradle. She got a glass of water for herself, then made her way back to the living room to figure out once and for all what exactly it was that her unexpected guest wanted.

13

"I have a question for you," Angie said as she sat down in the armchair across from Delphi. "Are you related to someone named Charlese Wilson? Her maiden name was Charlese McCray, which is why I ask."

The older woman nodded, a sad smile crossing her face. "Yes. She was my sister. She passed away two years ago. Lung cancer, and she never smoked a day in her life."

"I'm sorry," she said. "That's terrible."

"We weren't close until the last few years. I was a lot younger than her, you see. She had a hard life. She never remarried after her husband went missing, and when she started getting sick, she had no one else who could care for her. I'm grateful I was able to do so, though. We made our amends, for the most part."

"I'm sure she was glad to have you by her side," Angie said. "Pardon me asking, but did you ever marry? I'm just wondering because of your name."

Delphi chuckled. "Ah, yes, I'm still a McCray. Or rather, I'm a McCray again. My husband and I divorced when the kids left for college, and I changed my name back to my family name. My kids kept their father's name."

Angie nodded, then jumped into the subject she was really interested in. "So, did you come here to talk about your brother-in-law's watch?"

"You found it, then? It's really his?"

She nodded. "We got it cleaned up and were able to read the inscription on the back. I was actually looking up the names at the library earlier today. I should have recognized your name when you introduced yourself. I guess I was just thinking about too many things at once and it slipped by me."

Delphi gave her a short smile, but the expression quickly faded to one that Angie couldn't quite place. The older woman looked almost... scared. "Angie..."

Angie leaned forward as the other woman trailed off. Before Delphi could gird herself to speak again, the outdoor dogs took off on another round of barking.

Sighing, she pushed herself up from her seat. "I'd better go see what they're barking at."

"No!" The older woman's hand shot out and latched itself around Angie's arm in a vice-like grip. "It's too dangerous."

"What are you talking about?" Angie asked, trying and failing to snatch her arm away.

Delphi released her arm at last, only to lean close to Angie.

"It's my son," she whispered in a quavering voice. "Mikey's father. He's here for the watch, and if he thinks you know who it belonged to, he's going to kill you."

Angie stared at her for a long moment, trying to fit this new piece of information in with everything else she had learned about the mystery surrounding the old timepiece. "That doesn't make sense," she whispered. "He's too young to have had anything to do with Andy Wilson's disappearance back in the fifties."

Delphi gave her a look that was filled with such horror and sadness that it made Angie's skin crawl, but before she could say anything, Angie heard the sound of glass shattering from the rear of the house. Petunia gave a startled bark and stood up, her fur bristling.

"Where are you going?" she asked as Delphi stood up.

The older woman fixed her with a determined stare. "I'm going to go convince my son that he's making a terrible mistake. Wait here."

She strode down the hall, leaving Angie alone in the living room. She bit her lip, trying to decide what to do. Should she follow Delphi to make sure she was okay? Should she try to find something she could use to defend herself? Should she call the police?

In the end, she remained indecisive for too long. When she heard shouting from the other end of the house, her decision was made for her and she hurried down the hall, coming to a stop in her parents room. The window had been shattered, and shards of glass sparkled across the floor. Standing in the middle of the room was the man she recognized from the diner as Mikey's father. Delphi was standing only a few feet away from him, her hands held out placatingly.

"Don't do this, Mark. I'm done with all the lies."

"You were telling a different story last week," he said. His eyes flashed up to Angie. "Get out of my way, Ma. I'll take care of this."

He moved to walk around his mother, but she

stepped in his way again. "No! Don't hurt her, or I'll call the police on you myself."

This gave him pause, and he looked down at her in shock. "What in the world has gotten into you, Ma?"

The older woman shook her head. Angie could see tears in the corners of her eyes. She remained silent, however, and her son made to move her gently out of the way. His gaze, dark and angry, was fixed on Angie, who took a couple of steps back.

"What's going on?" she asked. Her voice came out shaky. "Delphi? I don't understand."

Delphi glanced back at her, then looked at her son again. She seemed to deflate. "I killed him. I killed Andy Wilson sixty years ago."

All three of them were silent for a long moment.

Mark was the first to break the silence. He reached out and practically lifted his mother off of her feet, moving her bodily to the side so that he could approach Angie, who backpedaled into the hallway, nearly tripping over Petunia. She was really regretting locking Oracle in the bathroom just then.

"All you had to do was give me the watch," Mark said as he approached her. "But no, you had to snoop. You had to get my mom involved in all of this. How did you lure her here? Did you find out her secret and threaten to tell the police?"

"I didn't know anything until five seconds ago," Angie said. "I swear. I won't tell anyone. Please, just leave me alone."

"Where's the watch? I know you found it. When my son came back to his seat that day in the diner and told me that the pretty woman with the good fries found a watch at the park we frequent, I knew right away what it was."

"How?" Angie asked, continuing to back down the hallway. Her fingers were buried in Petunia's scruff, and she was practically dragging the dog with her. Mark seemed wary of getting too close to the dog that had already chased him away once. "You wouldn't even have been born then."

"You're right. I was born about six months later. And I know every detail of what my father was wearing the day that he died. I've been searching for his body for years."

"Your father? I thought you were Delphi's son. She told me she and her husband got a divorce when her kids left for college."

"Andy Wilson was my father. The man who raised me, my mother's husband, married her when I was eighteen months old."

It took Angie a moment to figure it all out. That moment of hesitation was enough time for Mark to decide to brave Petunia's teeth. He lunged toward her, his hand coming close enough to brush her shirt as she stumbled back, pulling the husky with her. Petunia barked ferociously, but the dog had nothing on the elderly woman who suddenly shouted from behind Mark.

"Mark Smith, you leave that poor girl alone right now."

Mark turned and Angie could see his mother behind him, standing with her hands on her hips. She looked furious. Her gaze met Angie's and softened slightly.

"Yes, Mark is the result of an affair between myself and my sister's husband. Andy and I had been seeing each other in secret for a year before I found out I was pregnant. That fateful day was the day I decided to tell him. I made arrangements to meet him while he was out camping. He knew he'd be able to use fishing as an excuse to get away, since Charlese always hated the hobby. I convinced him to drive with me to our favorite park, and I told him under the willow tree where we had our first picnic. It was secluded, of course, since our affair was the best kept secret in the entire town." She sighed, suddenly looking very tired. "I was so young back then. So naive. I thought he'd leave my sister when he found out I was carrying his child. He didn't. He dumped me. Told me he'd deny everything if I ever told anyone. He offered me money to leave town, and told me he never wanted to see me again. I was hurt and I was angry. I was always an independent young woman, and so for my own safety I carried a small revolver in my purse. I pulled it out and shot him through the heart. Then I dragged his body into the forest as far as I could and drove back home and pretended I knew nothing."

"You never told anyone?" Angie whispered, her eyes wide.

"I told Mark," Delphi said, glancing toward her son. "When my sister passed away, I was... emotional. I think she knew, or at least suspected, that Mark was Andy's. She was always cold to him. He's the spitting image of his father. She never asked me though, and I never told her. But after she died, I had to tell someone, so I told my son the truth about who his father was. He knew the man who raised him wasn't his biological father, but he didn't ever know who was, not until a couple of years ago."

"And you didn't go straight to the police?" Angie asked, looking at Mark. "Your mother killed someone!"

"She killed someone over fifty years ago," he spat. "She never lifted a hand against anyone else. She was — and still is — an amazing mother and a good person. It took me a few days to come to terms with it, but then I devoted myself to finding his body. I wanted to make sure no one would ever be able to link the crime to her, or to our family. I made her tell me everything she could remember that might help me find him. And that watch was one of those things."

"Well, I don't have it anymore," Angie said. "I gave it to the police already. They'll figure everything out soon."

"It might be too late for the watch, but you know everything now. I'm sorry, Ma, but I'm not going to let her wreck our family."

With that he lunged at Angie, so quickly that she hardly had time to react. She stumbled backward, her foot catching on the edge of the hall rug. Her hand let go of Petunia's scruff reflexively, and as she went down the husky jumped forward, sinking her teeth into Mark's wrist. He shouted and jerked his hand back. From her perspective on the floor, Angie could see a bandage on his ankle and felt a surge of gratitude for her dog. Petunia had defended her against this man not once, but twice now.

Mark managed to pull his now bleeding wrist away from Petunia and kicked out at the dog. He missed, and Angie grabbed at Petunia to pull her away from him. Mark was glaring daggers at her, holding his injured wrist with his other hand.

Before he could make another move, a gut-wrenching scream came from behind him. He and Angie both looked in time to see his mother drop to the floor, clutching her chest.

"Ma!"

He twisted around and ran toward her, apparently either forgetting about Angie or deciding that his mother was more important than silencing her for good. Either way, Angie wasn't about to waste the chance to get out of there. She jumped up and started down the hallway toward the kitchen; a room that had a door that locked and a phone she could use to call the police.

As she hurried down the hallway, she turned to see Mark cradling his mother, who was slumped across his lap. As if sensing Angie's gaze on her, the older woman slitted her eyes open, met Angie's, and winked before pressing her hand to her chest again with a low groan.

EPILOGUE

"I've got to tell you, I don't think we've ever had a case like this," Detective O'Brien said. He looked tired, and gave his daughter an appreciative smile as she placed a plate chock full of ribs, mashed potatoes, and green beans in front of him.

Angie was over at the detective's house for dinner. Maggie and Joshua were there as well, though Josh was currently engaged with the video game console in the living room. Normally Maggie would make him eat at the table with the family, but tonight the adults wanted to talk without having to worry about impressionable ears listening in. Josh had only been too happy to eat his meal in front of the TV.

"I still can't believe that old lady faked a heart attack to save Angie," Maggie said.

"Don't remind me," Angie groaned. "I don't know how I'm supposed to feel about any of it. She killed someone. She had an affair with her sister's husband. She was a terrible person. But she may have saved my life, and she drove all the way out there just to stop her son from killing me. I don't even know why."

"We asked her," Detective O'Brien said, pausing between bites. "She said after you were so nice at the library, she just couldn't stand to see you get hurt. When she got back to the house she shares with her family, her daughter-in-law mentioned that Mark had gone out to 'work on his project,' which is what he called the search for the watch when speaking about it with Ms. McCray. She decided right then and there that she was done trying to cover up her trail."

"What's going to happen to her now?" Angie asked.

"I don't know yet. She'll be charged with second degree murder. She may be able to plea down from it, especially given the other circumstances. I don't think the judge will want to hand down a prison sentence to someone her age, someone who isn't a danger to society, unless he has no other choice. The fact that she's been cooperating – information she gave us helped us find the body, or at least what was left of the skeleton after fifty years. That's going to help her case a lot."

"What about Mark?" Maggie chimed in.

"Oh, we're throwing the book at him," her father said grimly. "We might be able to get him for attempted murder. With the death threat, and the fact that he had a knife concealed on his person, we can prove that he was planning on killing Angie. Mr. Miles is also going to be going against him in a civil suit, since Mark is the one who let his dogs go. He's looking at a long time behind bars, even if he gets a good lawyer."

"Good," Angie said firmly. "He deserves it. Delphi... Ms. McCray... I'm not so sure what I feel about her. She did something terrible. But she lived a good life afterward, and saved me. I guess I'm just glad this is all out of my hands now. Though I'll definitely be following the case."

"You'd be hard pressed not to," he said with a chuckle. "This is going to be talk of the town for months to come."

Angie winced, imagining the next day at the diner. She knew people were going to be all over her, asking for details about what exactly had happened. She supposed that was the price she paid for moving to a small town. Secrets always came to light eventually in Lost Bay.

ALSO BY PATTI BENNING

Papa Pacelli's Series

Book 1: Pall Bearers and Pepperoni

Book 2: Bacon Cheddar Murder

Book 3: Very Veggie Murder

Book 4: Italian Wedding Murder

Book 5: Smoked Gouda Murder

Book 6: Gourmet Holiday Murder

Book 7: Four Cheese Murder

Book 8: Hand Tossed Murder

Book 9: Exotic Pizza Murder

Book 10: Fiesta Pizza Murder

Book 11: Garlic Artichoke Murder

Book 12: On the Wings of Murder

Book 13: Mozzarella and Murder

Book 14: A Thin Crust of Murder

Book 15: Pretzel Pizza Murder

Book 16: Parmesan Pizza Murder

Book 17: Breakfast Pizza Murder

Book 18: Halloween Pizza Murder

Book 19: Thanksgiving Pizza Murder

Book 20: Christmas Pizza Murder

Book 21: A Crispy Slice of Murder

Book 22: Lobster Pizza Murder

Book 23: Pizza, Weddings, and Murder

Book 24: Pizza, Paradise, and Murder

Book 25: Meat Lovers and Murder

Book 26: Classic Crust Murder

Book 27: Hot, Spicy Murder

Book 28: Pork, Pizza, and Murder

Book 29: Chicken Alfredo Murder

Book 30: Jalapeño Pizza Murder

Book 31: Pesto Pizza Murder

Book 32: Sweet Chili Murder

Book 33: A Melted Morsel of Murder

Book 34: A Saucy Taste of Murder

Book 35: A Crunchy Crust of Murder

Book 36: Shrimply Sublime Murder

Darling Deli Series

Book 1: Pastrami Murder

Book 2: Corned Beef Murder

Book 3: Cold Cut Murder

Book 4: Grilled Cheese Murder

Book 5: Chicken Pesto Murder

Book 6: Thai Coconut Murder

Book 7: Tomato Basil Murder

Book 8: Salami Murder

Book 9: Hearty Homestyle Murder

Book 10: Honey BBQ Murder

Book 11: Beef Brisket Murder

Book 12: Garden Vegetable Murder

Book 13: Spicy Lasagna Murder

Book 14: Curried Lobster Murder

Book 15: Creamy Casserole Murder

Book 16: Grilled Rye Murder

Book 17: A Quiche to Die For

Book 18: A Side of Murder

Book 19: Wrapped in Murder

Book 20: Glazed Ham Murder

Book 21: Chicken Club Murder

Book 22: Pies, Lies and Murder

Book 23: Mountains, Marriage and Murder

Book 24: Shrimply Murder

Book 25: Gazpacho Murder

Book 26: Peppered with Murder

Book 27: Ravioli Soup Murder

Book 28: Thanksgiving Deli Murder

Book 29: A Season of Murder

Book 30: Valentines and Murder

Book 31: Shamrocks and Murder

Book 32: Sugar Coated Murder

Book 33: Murder, My Darling

Killer Cookie Series

Book 1: Killer Caramel Cookies

Book 2: Killer Halloween Cookies

Book 3: Killer Maple Cookies

Book 4: Crunchy Christmas Murder

Book 5: Killer Valentine Cookies

Asheville Meadows Series

Book 1: Small Town Murder

Book 2: Murder on Aisle Three

Book 3: The Heart of Murder

Book 4: Dating is Murder

Book 5: Dying to Cook

Book 6: Food, Family and Murder

Book 7: Fish, Chips and Murder

Book 8: Deathly Ever After

Cozy Tails of Alaska

Book 1: Mushing is Murder

Book 2: Murder Befalls Us

Standalones

Tall, Dark, and Deadly

A Merry Little Murder

AUTHOR'S NOTE

I'd love to hear your thoughts on my books, the storylines, and anything else that you'd like to comment on—reader feedback is very important to me. My contact information, along with some other helpful links, is listed below. If you'd like to be on my list of "folks to contact" with updates, release and sales notifications, etc.... just shoot me an email and let me know. Thanks for reading!

Also...

... if you're looking for more great reads, I am proud to announce that Summer Prescott Books publishes several popular series by Cozy authors Summer Prescott and Gretchen Allen, as well as Allyssa Mirry, Carolyn Q. Hunter, Blair Merrin, Susie Gayle and more!

CONTACT SUMMER PRESCOTT BOOKS PUBLISHING

Twitter: @summerprescott1

Blog and Book Catalog: http://summerprescottbooks.com

Email: summer.prescott.cozies@gmail.com

And…look up The Summer Prescott Fan Page and Summer Prescott Publishing Page on Facebook – let's be friends!

To download a free book, and sign up for our fun and exciting newsletter, which will give you opportunities to win prizes and swag, enter contests, and be the first to know about New Releases, click here: http://summerprescottbooks.com